Heidi's Song

Beaver Boo

First published in Great Britain in 1983 by
The Hamlyn Publishing Group Limited
London · New York · Sydney · Toronto
Astronaut House, Feltham, Middlesex, England

© Copyright 1983 Hanna-Barbera Productions Inc
ISBN 0 600 20784 6

Printed and bound in Great Britain by
Cox & Wyman Limited, Reading

Although she doesn't play a very important part in this story, Aunt Dete always insisted that if it hadn't been for her, nothing at all would have happened, and Heidi's life would have been very different. Grandfather disagreed with Aunt Dete, but then Grandfather always disagreed with everything Aunt Dete said. Who was right? As our story unfolds, you can decide for yourself.

It is a warm and sunny June morning in Switzerland. Two figures are to be seen crossing a flower-strewn upland meadow.

Once across the meadow, they will make their way up a narrow trail which climbed the mountainside. Even at a distance, the difference in their sizes is enough to tell that one is a grown-up young woman and the other a very young girl.

Not long after their ascent of the steep trail began, an observer would have noticed that the larger of the two figures was losing ground. In a very short time, the child was far in front, as the adult paused more and more frequently to catch her breath. From time to time she grasped at her heavy skirt and clutched at her inappropriately large hat with the long drooping feather flopping about on the brim. When the young girl was far enough in front so that she was completely out of sight of her companion, she sat down on a convenient stone, removed her shoes, stockings, hat, coat and top dress.

"Phew!" she exclaimed aloud, even though there was no one to hear her. "That's a lot better! Aunt Dete had me so bundled up I could hardly breathe!" Then she piled her discarded clothes neatly by the

side of the trail and continued on her way up.

She hadn't gone very far when she saw a herd of goats above her on the mountain. One very young coal-black kid had wandered away from the herd, in hot pursuit of a butterfly.

Still higher on the mountainside, a keen-eyed hawk perched in a tree, watching every move of the herd, but paying especially close attention to the antics of the unsuspecting young goat. Finally, in greedy anticipation of an easy kill, the hawk launched himself in a swooping dive, sure that the black kid had wandered so far there would be no escape for him.

The young goat didn't realize he was in trouble until the hawk, cruel talons reaching and deadly beak poised to strike, was almost upon him. A frantic, twisting leap to one side surprised the hawk, but not for long, as the evil bird turned in mid-air and continued his attack. Then the kid began ducking, dodging, twisting and turning to avoid becoming a meal for the hungry hawk.

Even though the young goat was inexperienced, instinct and agility were working in his favour. The turning and dodging were always in the direction of the herd of goats, as he attempted to work his way back to the safety of the herd. Still, the struggle was so one-sided that it could end in only one way: with the hawk carrying off the kid, to devour him at leisure. Suddenly, however, a new element entered the battle in the form of Great Turk, a huge ram with an immense spread of dangerous-looking horns, who was the leader of the herd.

When Great Turk came charging at the hawk, the bird knew he was going to go hungry, at least so far as the black kid was concerned. He made one last desperate strike but was forced to pull up short and dive away, as Great Turk planted himself firmly in front of the little goat, defying the hawk to continue the attack. The big bird finally gave up and flew back to his perch to watch and wait for an easier prey.

All this while, the young girl had been climbing steadily up the trail. Far below her, Aunt Dete suddenly realized that she

had lost sight of the child. Immediately panic-stricken, because she knew well all the unfortunate things which could befall a young child in mountain country, she began to call to her. When she had called urgently several times without any answer, she drew one tremendous breath and, using every bit of her considerable lung power, let loose a tremendous yell!

"HEEEIIIDDIII!" Aunt Dete's cry was so loud that echoes sprang from peak to peak, gathering force with each echo.

On the trail, Heidi had reached the herd of goats, which was tended by the goatherd, a young boy named Peter. When the sturdy sturdy blond child came into view, Peter stared at her, then at the goats, then at the mountains. He listened to the echos of Aunt Dete's superpowerful yell bouncing from peak to peak, looked again at the girl and called, "You there! What's a Heidi?"

"I'm Heidi," said the girl. "Who are you, and where did you get all those nice sheep?"

"I'm Peter," the boy replied. "And they're not sheep—they're goats, as anybody with eyes can plainly see!"

"Oh," said Heidi. "I didn't know." Then, pointing to the small black kid, she asked, "What's that one's name? She's cute. Would she make a nice pet?"

"Oh, phooey!" snorted Peter. "That's Spritz—and he's a he, not a she! And I don't think he'd make a very good pet—he has bad manners and gets into mischief!"

"Do all of them belong to you?" Heidi asked.

"Of course not!" Peter answered. "I tend them for people—take them to graze in the early morning and bring them back in the late afternoon." Then he looked hard at Heidi, walked all around her and said, "You're not from anywhere around here, are you?"

"No," replied Heidi. "I'm not from around here—but I'm going to be. I've come to live with my grandfather."

"Your grandfather? Why don't you live with your mother and father?" Peter asked.

Heidi's face clouded, and for a moment Peter thought she might burst into tears. Then she said quietly, "My mother and father are in heaven."

Peter looked as embarrassed as he felt. Then he frowned and asked, "Is your grandfather the old bear who lives up there?" pointing to the cabin near the top of the Wunderhorn.

"I suppose so," Heidi answered. "Aunt Dete said he lived high up on this trail. But what do you mean, 'the old bear'? That's what Aunt Dete called him, too."

"Oh," said Peter, "he's a bear all right. Always in a temper, growls all the time, never says a kind word to anybody at all. Some of these goats belong to him—Spritz is one of them. He makes cheese and butter from the goats' milk and sells them in Dorfli, the village where I live."

"I know about Dorfli," Heidi said. "We passed it on the way up. We started from the village where I've been living with Aunt Dete since my mother and father went to heaven. I'd better be getting up to meet my grandfather now. Good-bye, Peter. Maybe we'll see each other soon."

"I'll go along with you," Peter said. "I'm taking the goats up to pasture—and I'm a little late."

As they moved up the trail, with the goats trailing behind, Heidi began asking Peter questions.

"Have you always lived in Dorfli?" "How old are you?" "Do you go to school?" "Who do you live with?"

After Peter had answered, "Yes," "Eleven," "Sometimes," and finally, "With my mother and grandmother," he pointed up the trail and said, "There he is—the old bear himself!"

Heidi looked where Peter was pointing. She saw a big, strong-looking old man, with white hair, a white beard, and huge, bushy gray eyebrows. His face was deeply lined, and he wore a shirt open at the neck, a leather vest, and rough trousers tucked into leather boots. He was leaning on the handle of his ax. Beside him sat his dog Gruffle, a large shaggy hound who, if the truth were told, looked a little like his master.

"You, there—Peter!" the old man boomed in a voice so deep it seemed to come from his toes. "Where have you been—you're late! Get those goats moving!" Then he looked at Heidi and said, "What's this? No little girls

allowed up here—back down the trail with you!"

Heidi began to reply, "But, Grandfather, I have to—"

The old man frowned and roared, "Grandfather? Why do you call me Grandfather?"

"Because that's who you are—her grandfather!" angrily said Aunt Dete, who had just huffed and puffed her way to the cabin.

"Just a minute!" said Grandfather, glaring at Aunt Dete. "I know who you are! You're the sister of my son's wife!"

"That's right," snipped Aunt Dete. "Your son is dead, and so is my sister. I've taken care of the child for the last four years—now it's your turn!"

"Oh, no you don't!" yelled Grandfather. "You can just take the child and march back down the trail in your silly long skirt and your ridiculous hat with that stupid feather flopped about!"

"Oh, I'll go back down all right," replied Aunt Dete, "but Heidi stays here. I have a good job waiting for me in a resort hotel, and I can no longer look after her. I say again—it's your turn!"

The old man looked even more furious. "My turn? MY TURN! You think this is some sort of game?" Then he looked again at Heidi, and his expression softened just a little.

"You!" he barked.

"Yes, Grandfather?" Heidi said.

"Do you cry?" he said.

"No, Grandfather," replied Heidi.

"Good," he roared. "I can't stand little girls who cry!"

"Do you get all sulky and stand about in corners?" he demanded.

"No, Grandfather," answered Heidi.

"Very good!" he said. "Little sulky girls have no place here! Last question: Do you eat a lot?"

"I'm afraid so, Grandfather," replied Heidi. "I get hungry!"

"Excellent!" Grandfather growled. "I hate little girls with no appetite!" He looked Heidi up and down, walked around her and finally said, "Well! I suppose if one had children, one can expect also to have grandchildren! Peter, why are you standing there with your foolish mouth open? Get on up to

the pasture with the goats!" Then, turning to Aunt Dete, he roared, "Get out of my sight, woman—and don't come back! I'll keep the child—but I want no more of you!"

Aunt Dete tried to be brave as she said, "Be assured, old man, I want no more of you either." She threw Heidi's discarded clothes at his feet and ran panic-stricken down the trail.

Grandfather reached out his big hand and took Heidi's small one. "Good riddance to her!" he said. "Come, and we'll go up to the cabin. I don't think it's going to work, but we have to try, even though this is no place for little girls."

"We'll make it work, Grandfather! Just wait and see!" Heidi replied.

"Yes," Grandfather said, "we will, indeed, see. Are you hungry now?"

Heidi said, "It's been a long time since breakfast!"

"Would toasted cheese and fresh-baked bread and a bowl of milk help you to stop being hungry?" When Grandfather asked this, there was something that looked suspiciously like a twinkle in his eye.

A little later, after they had reached

Grandfather's cabin and Heidi had eaten, she began to look around, curious to learn more about the place in which she was going to live.

"Grandfather isn't a very good housekeeper," she thought. The cabin was furnished with the barest of necessities: a bed, a table, a chair, several stools, a sink for washing up and a woodburning stove which served for cooking and heating. While nothing was really dirty, there was dust everywhere, and even some cobwebs where spiders had been busy in the corners. Against one wall was a closet. Without thinking very much about it, Heidi reached to open the closet doors.

Grandfather, who was sharpening his ax, saw what Heidi was trying to do out of the corner of his eye and cried out in alarm.

"No!" he shouted. "Don't!"

Unfortunately, he was a little too late. By that time, Heidi had the closet doors open and, because everything in the closet, including all of Grandfather's clothes, tools, books, canned goods and a lot of other things, had been simply jammed and

crammed inside instead of being hung up or neatly assorted and stacked or piled, the entire contents came tumbling out, nearly knocking Heidi down.

"*Ach!*" groaned Grandfather. "You see? I told you it wouldn't work. You're here only a few minutes, and you've upset everything because you had to poke your nose into my closet!"

"I'm sorry, Grandfather," Heidi replied. "I'll get it all back in the closet again—but I'm going to make it neat and tidy inside when I do!"

"*Ach!*" groaned Grandfather again, but louder this time. "You do that, and I'll never be able to find anything in there!"

Heidi didn't answer Grandfather's last remark. Instead, she continued to look around the cabin. Finally, she turned to the old man and asked, "Grandfather, there's only one bed here. Where am I going to sleep?"

"In the hayloft," he replied.

Gazing around, Heidi noticed a ladder leading to what looked like a shelf high up in the cabin. She climbed the ladder and looked about.

"Oh, my!" she exclaimed. "This is nice! I'll like sleeping high up, and the hay is fresh and smells so sweet! And there's even a window—I can open it and look right out at the stars!"

"Well," said Grandfather to himself, "at least she knows how to make the best of a situation!"

Later, after a simple supper, Heidi and Grandfather prepared for bed.

"Isn't there a lot of wind tonight?" Heidi asked. "It's whistling and making all kinds of howling noises!"

"Some of it is the wind," Grandfather said. "I'm afraid we may have a storm. And if we do, the kobolds and erlkings and all manner of creatures will be out tonight!"

"Wh—wh—what are kobolds and erlkings?" asked Heidi.

"Those who don't know better really think it is just the wind," Grandfather replied. "But those of us who live on the Wunderhorn know that the kobolds and erlkings, along with a lot of others, are strange mountain creatures who live in dark, mysterious places. All of them will be out to-

night, because two strangers have invaded their mountains—and one of the invaders is still here—right in my cabin!"

"But, Grandfather," Heidi said, "wouldn't they know I'm not an invader—I'm your granddaughter!"

"Oh," replied Grandfather, nodding his head solemnly and shaking his white beard, "who knows what a kobold thinks? And besides, there are all the others!"

"The—the others?" gasped Heidi.

"Certainly!" Grandfather said, in his deepest voice. "Besides the kobolds and erlkings, there are the boggles and boggarts, the gepolter, the erdgeists, the teufelcher, the bardghests, the afreets and the trolls, not to mention the harpies and the jinns. And over all of them is the King of the Kobolds! He is almost as big as a mountain! His legs are as big as the biggest trees, and his arms could crush a whole village! His beard is long, like green moss, and his eyes flash like the lightning!"

"Oh, my!" Heidi said. "I don't think I'd like to meet him!"

"Don't worry," Grandfather said. "He

would pay you no attention at all—you are not important enough! Now—off to bed with you!"

Heidi went up the ladder to her bedroom in the hayloft. She put on her nightclothes, and when Grandfather blew out the candles, she opened her window and looked outside.

Clouds streamed through the sky, chased by the wind. When the clouds allowed moonlight to break through, Heidi could see the wind-blown trees bending almost double. From time to time, lightning streaked across the night sky, lighting up the wild mountain scene.

Very soon, Heidi fell into a dream-filled sleep. In her dream, the wind seemed to be calling her: "HEEEIIIDDDIII! COMMMME OOOUUUTTT AND PLAAAY WITH US!"

Heidi did what the wind asked. It seemed to her that she simply floated out of her window, where she was greeted by an army of the weird mountain creatures about which Grandfather had warned.

All about her, thunder rumbled like an angry bear awakened from its winter nap, and lightning flashed on either side. The wind's howl became a shriek.

Heidi thought all of the creatures were wonderful. She watched one group which looked like long clouds with brightly lit tails and then another group floated by which, to Heidi, looked like crocodiles with human heads.

Then, as still others went by in a weird procession, she thought, "Those look silly— just a lot of sparks—like fireworks that keep jumping around! Oh! Oh, my!" She clapped her hands in delight.

Then, a flock of wind harpies descended. Diving and circling through the wild sky, they rapidly surrounded Heidi. She thought they were beautiful until they got closer and she saw that, in spite of their pale blue gowns, filmy wings, and long hair, they had hideous white skulls where women's faces should have been.

Heidi began to frolic with all of the strange and wonderful creatures, tumbling about, swooping, whirling and soaring in and around the mountain peaks. She was enjoying all of this playful dashing about until she saw a fearsome giant, the King of the Kobolds.

He looked exactly as Grandfather had described him. She stared wide-eyed at his hair, a tangled mass of thorny vines, and at his beard of slimy moss. He glared at Heidi and angrily pointed a long gnarled finger at her. Suddenly, the frolicking wasn't fun any more. Instead of playing, all the creatures seemed to be angry and, without any warning, they began chasing her through the sky, in and around the mountain peaks. She ran as fast as she could, but the creatures kept gaining on her.

She didn't know what she was going to do, but thought that if she got back to Grandfather's cabin, he would be able to help her.

She stopped her swooping and swirling and headed through the sky in a beeline for the cabin, with the night creatures screeching and howling in hot pursuit. Just as the closest of the creatures was about to catch her, she sailed through her open window, slammed it shut, pulled the covers over her ears and—woke up to a magnificently sunny and warm morning!

With great relief, Heidi looked around and saw that all was as it should be.

She went downstairs and had some breakfast, then went outside to enjoy the beautiful day. In the distance she could hear the goats, as they came up the trail with Peter. Close by, she heard the "thunk" of an axe being swung lustily at a tree. Heidi walked toward the sound of the "thunks." At the top of a tall tree, she saw an owl, sitting on a branch, saying "Whooo."

"Hello, there!" she called to the owl. "You say 'Who' so much, I'm going to call you Hootie." Then she noticed Grandfather chopping away at the foot of Hootie's tree.

"Grandfather!" Heidi shouted. "Stop!"

She ran for the tree crying, "Hootie! Fly off! The tree's going to fall!" But the owl paid no attention.

Then, with a great CRRACK, the mighty tree began to fall. Heidi ran even faster to where she thought the top of the tree would fall. Unfortunately, she didn't run fast enough to be clear of the tree.

Grandfather dashed toward Heidi and gave her a tremendous shove, just as the tree dropped. She almost flew through the air, but she got out of the way of the tree just in time . . . and Hootie dropped right into her arms.

After carefully placing Hootie on the low branch of a tree, Heidi turned to look for Grandfather. He had not been as lucky as Heidi. The tree had fallen with a loud rumble that shook the earth for miles around, and when the forest was still again, Heidi had called out to him several times, and got no answer.

Frantically, she began to search. Peter, who had seen what happened as he came up the trail, came to help.

"Peter!" wailed Heidi. "I can't find Grandfather anywhere! I'm sure the tree fell on him after he pushed me out of the way!"

Peter began to look for Grandfather and soon discovered a booted foot between two branches. He pulled some branches aside, then called to Heidi, "I've found him! Over here!"

Breathlessly, Heidi ran to where Peter stood. Together they pulled the smaller branches from the huge limb under which Grandfather was pinned. At last, they had removed everything but the biggest part of the branch, under which Grandfather's leg was painfully trapped.

Grandfather lay motionless, with his eyes tightly closed.

"Heidi," Peter whispered, "I think he's dead."

"Dead!" the figure on the ground snorted. "Who's dead? Nonsense!"

Heidi shouted joyfully, "Thank goodness you're all right, Grandfather!"

"All right!" Grandfather roared. "How can I be all right when a tree fell on my leg? Get this tree off me and help me back to the cabin!"

After much grunting and straining, Peter and Heidi managed to get Grandfather out from under the tree. With him leaning heavily on both of them, they worked their way back to the cabin, where Grandfather collapsed on his bed with a loud groan.

"Oh!" he moaned. "I don't deserve this.

I've been chopping down trees all my life, and this is the first time I've ever had an accident! And all because, out of the goodness of my heart, I took in an eight-year-old orphan child!"

"Don't worry, Grandfather!" Heidi said. "Peter will fetch the doctor from the village."

"THERE WILL BE NO DOCTOR IN MY HOUSE!" thundered the old man. "My leg is not broken. I'll be fine in the morning after some rest."

"Well, then!" Heidi said. "I'll just look after you myself. I'll do the cleaning and milk the goats and cook your meals. Peter can help too!"

"This is what I meant when I told you it wouldn't work!" growled Grandfather. "You'll do the cleaning—and then I'll never find anything! You'll milk the goats—and we'll have sour milk. You'll cook the meals—and we'll all have indigestion."

"You musn't worry, Grandfather," Heidi said. "Everything will be all right. You'll see."

"Yes, I'm sure I'll see," snapped Grandfather. "And while I'm waiting to see, young lady, can you tell me what happened to that

foolish owl you were so busy trying to save? He's the cause of all this trouble."

"He's outside now," Peter said. "I think he's sort of adopted Heidi because she tried to save him."

In the morning, Grandfather's leg was still very sore. He stayed in bed all that day complaining about anything and everything.

Until Grandfather's leg healed, Heidi did all the chores as she had promised. She cleaned the cabin till it shone and cooked the meals. Peter came to milk the goats before they went to pasture, and when he brought them back at night, he helped with the churning.

Heidi grew to love the mountains and especially her gruff Grandfather. Grandfather was also quite pleased with Heidi, although, of course, he didn't tell her.

After several days, Grandfather was limping about, using an old stick. One morning, several weeks later, Heidi came into the cabin with two pails brimming with milk.

"Look, Grandfather!" she exclaimed. "I've milked the goats all by myself!"

Grandfather peeked into the pails. "That's

very good, Heidi!" he said. "Most people don't get that much milk the first time they try it!"

"Now, maybe I'll learn to tend the whole herd!" Heidi said.

"Better begin with just one," Grandfather cautioned. "I'll give you Spritz. You can learn with him!"

"Oh, Grandfather!" cried Heidi. "You mean I can have Spritz for my very own?"

"Of course that's what I mean!" roared Grandfather. "I just said so, didn't I?"

"My goodness!" Heidi exclaimed. "A goat for my very own! I can't wait to tell Peter!"

"You won't have to wait very long," Grandfather said. "I can hear him coming up the trail with the goats!"

Heidi dashed outside and ran down the trail to meet Peter. "Peter!" she called. "Grandfather gave me Spritz! Gave him to me to keep!"

"I don't believe it!" Peter answered. "Gave you Spritz? Heidi, that old grouch never gave anybody anything! You'll have to prove it to me!"

"If Grandfather tells you it's so—then will you believe it?" Heidi asked.

"I suppose so," Peter replied.

"Then let's go right to the cabin!" Heidi said. "He'll tell you!"

The two children, followed by the goat herd, raced back up the trail to the cabin, where Grandfather was standing in the doorway.

"Grandfather!" Heidi shouted. "Peter doesn't believe that you gave Spritz to me! Will you please tell him?"

"Certainly I'll tell him!" Grandfather said. "Peter, I gave Spritz to Heidi. Does that satisfy you, young man?"

"I don't know about Peter," Heidi said, "but it satisfies me!" Then she looked more closely at Grandfather and said, "I see something that's even more satisfying! Grandfather, you're not using your cane! You can get about just like you used to before the tree fell on your legs!"

Grandfather looked down at his legs, then at his hands. "What do you know!" he said in wonderment. "I didn't even notice! Now maybe we can get things back to normal around here and have a little celebration!" But then he happened to look down the trail

and growled, "We'll have to postpone the celebration for a while. Here comes that woman again, bringing trouble with her, no doubt."

Heidi looked down the trail and exclaimed, "Aunt Dete! I wonder what she wants?"

"Nothing good, I'll bet," Grandfather said. As Aunt Dete approached the cabin, Grandfather roared at her, "I told you before—I'll tell you again—I want no more of you up here! Back down the trail with you, woman!"

Aunt Dete paused to catch her breath. Then she said, "I will go back down the trail happily, old man! As a matter of fact, I would go almost anywhere to get out of the sight of you! But when I go, I will take Heidi with me!"

"What?" roared Grandfather. "You will do nothing of the kind! You have gone mad, woman, mad at last! Heidi stays here!"

"I'm no more mad than you, you—you— OLD BEAR!" Aunt Dete shrieked. "And I'm smart enough to know that up here on the Wunderhorn, Heidi will remain an ignoramus—she will never learn anything!

Knowing you and your stubborn ways, I'll bet you won't even send her to school! But in Frankfurt, there is a very wealthy man with a daughter—a young girl—who is an invalid. He would very much like to have Heidi come to live with them and be a companion to his daughter."

"But, Aunt Dete," exclaimed Heidi, "I'm just getting used to the life up here, and Grandfather has given me Spritz to keep for myself!"

"What is that compared to the opportunity for you in Frankfurt?" replied Aunt Dete. "Heidi, you are simply too young to be able to make such a decision for yourself! Besides, in Frankfurt you will learn to read and write and do sums, and you will have the chance to associate with cultured and important people and grow up to be a fine lady!"

"Can I take Spritz with me?" Heidi asked.

"Foolish child—of course not!" replied Aunt Dete. "Such an animal wouldn't even be allowed in Frankfurt, let alone in the Sesemann household!"

Heidi turned to the white-bearded old

man. "I don't want to go, Grandfather," she cried. "Can't I stay here with you?"

"I don't like any of this!" snorted Grandfather. "I didn't want you to begin with—but now, when I'm used to you, and we are beginning to enjoy each other, my life goes topsy-turvy again!"

"Just as I thought!" Aunt Dete snorted. "You care only about yourself and not at all about the good fortune that has come Heidi's way."

Grandfather glared at Aunt Dete. He paused for a moment, then turned to Heidi and said, "Much as I hate to admit it, Heidi, your Aunt Dete is probably right. Here you will grow up strong and healthy, but in Frankfurt you will have an opportunity to learn about things most people consider important. I don't want you to go, but I suppose it is for the best."

"You see?" Aunt Dete said. "Your Grandfather agrees with me—wonder of wonders—so it must be the right thing to do."

"I'm not going," Heidi said. "This is my home. I love it here. I can't leave Grandfather and Spritz and . . . ."

Aunt Dete interrupted her. "You heard what the old man said. Now go quickly and put on your best dress for the trip to Frankfurt."

Soon Heidi had changed into the clothes she had worn on the day she'd climbed the mountain for the first time. The brim of her old hat couldn't hide the tears on her face.

Heidi begged Aunt Dete one last time to let her stay, but Aunt Dete grabbed Heidi's hand and began to run down the trail, dragging Heidi behind her.

In the last of many sorrowful backward looks, Heidi saw that Peter had joined Grandfather at the cabin. With his arm around Peter's shoulders, Grandfather, staring straight ahead and blinking hard, silently raised his hand in farewell. Peter waved, turning away as he wiped his eyes on his sleeve.

All the animals were sadly quiet and seemed to sense that Heidi was leaving. High overhead Hootie circled, watching as Heidi and Aunt Dete stumbled down the mountainside. In fact, he followed them every inch of the way from the Wunderhorn to Frankfurt.

Peter and Grandfather returned to work, already missing Heidi and wondering if they would ever see her again.

After a long trip, Heidi and Aunt Dete finally reached the bustling city which was their destination.

As they rode through the city, Heidi stared in wonder at everything: the traffic on the busy streets, the stores and shops, warehouses and office buildings, parks and fine homes. Tall buildings crowded the clouds, while street vendors and factory whistles drowned out the songs of birds.

Soon, the carriage rattled to a halt. In front of Heidi was a home more imposing than all the others she had seen along the way.

"Here we are," said Aunt Dete. "This is your new home."

Heidi gasped. This huge, gloomy pile of brick and stone was to be her home? There were dozens of windows and small porches on each of the three floors. Already, she missed Grandfather's tiny cottage.

"My goodness," Heidi exclaimed. "It's so big—and looks so lonely!"

"You'll soon get over that feeling," Aunt Dete said. "Now mind your manners and stand up straight!" They started up the broad steps to the great front door with the lion's-head knocker. Boom! Boom! Boom! The huge brass knocker made a dreadful clamour as it struck the door. It seemed to warn Heidi that she didn't belong here.

The door swung open and there stood a tall and very overweight man. The stiff collar of his dark uniform came almost to his ears, so that his bald head looked like a large melon resting on a table. His face looked quite red and angry.

The butler sneered down his hooked nose at the visitors and said loudly, "I am Sebastian, the butler. What do you want?"

"I have brought the child to be companion to the invalid young lady of the house," replied Aunt Dete.

Sebastian looked at Heidi scornfully. "This is what you have brought? Hah! Frau Rottenmeir will take one look at her and order her out instantly! "Then he pointed to Aunt Dete and barked, "You! Wait here!" Glaring at Heidi, he ordered, "And you—

you insignificant pipsqueak, come with me! Wipe your feet! Stay close behind me! Touch nothing! And, above all, speak only when you are spoken to!" Then he slammed the door in Aunt Dete's face and led the way into the house and down a long gloomy hall.

"Pay attention," Sebastian said, as they walked down the hall. "When Frau Rottenmeir speaks—you will listen. There is to be no speaking back!" Heidi was having some trouble understanding Sebastian, because of his heavy German accent.

Coming toward them in the hall was a very pretty, young woman in a maid's uniform. She stopped when she saw Sebastian and Heidi.

"Oh, Sebastian," she said. "This must be the little girl who's to be the companion. What's your name, little girl?"

"I'm Heidi, Frau Rottenmeir," she replied.

"FRAU ROTTENMEIR?" roared Sebastian. "Stupid girl! Do you know NOTHING? This is only Tinette, a housemaid! Come!"

They continued down the long hall until finally they came to a doorway. Sebastian opened the door and, followed by Heidi,

stepped into a large room overflowing with dark heavy furniture. Thick drapes at the windows blocked the sun and made Heidi yearn for the openness of her mountain home.

In the centre of the room stood a tall, thin woman who reminded Heidi of a pointed stick, made black and brittle in a fire. Frau Rottenmeir stood stiffly, in a severe black dress, with her hair pulled back into a tight knot. Heidi could tell at a glance that this frightening woman was already furious with her. As she timidly approached, the housekeeper began to tap her toe sharply and to shake her head. Even Schnoodle, the nasty little dachshund in Frau Rottenmeir's arms, snarled.

"She is called Heidi—," replied Sebastian. "She is to be companion to Clara."

"This one is not worthy to be a companion to Schnoodle!" Frau Rottenmeir said. "I have never seen such insignificance. She is a nothing—nothing at all! You will see that she is shipped back to the woods or mountains or maybe to the zoo! Tinette!" This

last word was a loud shriek. Immediately the door opened and Tinette entered.

"Take her away at once!" Frau Rottenmeir ordered. "Sebastian, we may have to disinfect the house!" She gave Heidi one more scornful look and finished by stamping her foot and shouting, "Begone!"

From behind the drapes at one of the windows came a voice. "No! I don't want her to go!" And then the drapes parted, and a young girl in a wheelchair propelled herself to the little group in the centre of the room.

The girl in the chair was quite attractive, but her cheeks were pale, and she looked very frail. She wore a pretty white dress trimmed with lace. She wheeled the chair up to Heidi and said, "Hello! I'm Clara. We're going to be good friends, aren't we?"

"I hope so," replied Heidi. "My name is Heidi—but I don't think your mother wants me to stay!"

"My mother?" said Clara. "Indeed, I wish my dear mother could have been here. She would have greeted you warmly." Then, as a sad look clouded her pretty face, she said gently, "My mother is dead."

"I'm sorry," replied Heidi. "So is mine— and my father, too!"

"Then I suppose I am more fortunate than you," Clara said. "My father travels a great deal on business, but he writes to me almost every day. I will show you some of his letters, if you like."

"That will be very nice," Heidi answered. "Maybe you will read them to me?"

"There! You see!" Frau Rottenmeir interjected. "She is obviously a very stupid creature! She cannot even read! She is obviously not fit for this household!"

"Nonsense!" replied Clara. "She's like a breath of fresh air in this stuffy old house— and I'll have someone to talk to! Heidi, this unpleasant person is Frau Rottenmeir, our housekeeper."

Frau Rottenmeir looked very angry at this. "Very well, Miss Clara, if you insist," she almost snarled. "But your father will hear of this upon his return! Tinette—take her to her room, and see that she is scrubbed before she sleeps!"

Heidi followed Tinette into the long hall, then up a broad staircase and down another hall to an open door. Heidi stepped into the

room and looked around in wonderment at the handsome furniture and drapes.

"My goodness!" she exclaimed as she looked at the bed. "I don't think I'll be able to sleep in here—I never slept in a bed with a roof on it!"

Tinette laughed. "Silly! It's only curtains—it's called a canopy bed. You'll be asleep before you know it!"

"But it's so quiet!" Heidi said. "I'm used to hearing goats bleating and owls hooting and Grandfather snoring!"

"Try counting sheep jumping over a fence!" laughed Tinette.

"I'm more used to goats," Heidi replied. "Do you suppose I could count them?"

"You could count alligators or elephants or whales, if you wish! Good night, Heidi!" said Tinette, as she went out the door.

Heidi changed into her nightclothes and went to the window to look out. She couldn't see him, but her friend from the Wunderhorn, Hootie the owl, was perched in a tall tree in the backyard, keeping an eye on things. The last thing Heidi heard before she fell asleep was Hootie's repeated cry of "Whoooo! Whoooo! Whoooo!"

In the morning, Heidi got out of bed and went to another window in her bedroom. She saw a horse-drawn wagon pulled up to the front of the house. A very pleasant-looking, strong young man directed a chute from the wagon into the cellar window. With a loud clatter, coal began tumbling down the chute. On the steps, Tinette watched with interest. But it was obvious that Tinette's interest was in the young man, not his horse and wagon full of coal.

"Good morning, Willi!" called the pretty, young housemaid.

"Good morning, Miss Tinette," replied Willi.

"My, you must be very strong to shovel all that coal so easily!" Tinette said gaily.

Willi began his reply by blushing furiously at the compliment, then muttered something which sounded like, "Oh, I'm not so very strong!"

Tinette, who was enjoying herself, said, "What did you say, Willi? I didn't hear you!"

Willi gulped once, then blurted, "I said I am not so strong as my horse!" Then, as he

started to blush again, he bent over and made the coal fairly fly with his shovel.

"I don't suppose you ever go walking when you finish delivering your coal?" Tinette asked, with a look she hoped was innocent—and charming.

"Oh, yes," replied Willi. "When I finish the coal, I always walk with Gretchen!"

At this, Tinette stamped her foot in exasperation. "With Gretchen!" she exclaimed. "Well! I certainly hope you enjoy your walk, Mr. Coal-dust Dirty-face Willi!" Then she went into the house, slamming the front door with a crash.

Heidi leaned out of her window in time to hear Willi say, "What did I SAY? What did I DO??"

"Willi," called Heidi. "Don't be upset— Tinette likes you—I could tell!"

"How can she like me?" groaned Willi. "She called me Coal-dust Dirty-face and slammed the door at me!"

"Don't you worry," Heidi said. "I know she likes you. She just didn't like you walking with another young lady—that Gretchen!"

"Gretchen?" Willi said. "Certainly I walk with Gretchen—to the stables after my work is done! Gretchen is my horse!"

"Well, then!" Heidi said. "There's nothing to fret about, is there? As soon as Tinette finds out about Gretchen, everything will be all right, because she likes you!"

"Well, I like her, too," replied Willi. "But what can I do? I think I would maybe even like to marry her! But I'm afraid of girls—especially pretty ones like Tinette!"

"I'll see what I can do," Heidi began, but had to break off because there was a loud knocking at her door. Heidi hurried to the door and opened it. Sebastian stood there, frowning and trying to look important at the same time.

"You will dress at once and follow me!" barked Sebastian.

Heidi dressed in a hurry, and they began a long walk through the halls and downstairs and upstairs and through more halls. As they walked, Heidi began to ask questions.

"Where are we going, Mr. Sebastian?" was the first question.

"It is time for you to join Miss Clara to keep her company," Sebastian answered.

"Oh," said Heidi. She thought for a moment and then asked, "How did Clara get hurt? Why doesn't she walk, instead of rolling around in that wheelchair?"

"This is not a subject for you to talk about!" snapped Sebastian. "Clara is not hurt—she is just not well. But you must not speak of this matter again!" Sebastian's face looked even redder than usual.

A few moments later, they arrived at the door to Clara's room. Sebastian knocked, and Clara's voice called, "Come in!"

Sebastian opened the door, and they walked in. "I have brought you this—this Heidi creature for company!" he said.

"Come right in, Heidi!" said Clara. "Sebastian, that will be all—you may go." Sebastian clicked his heels and left.

"Please sit by me, Heidi," Clara said. "I have just dozens of questions I want to ask you!" Heidi pulled up a chair, sat down and replied, "There are so many things I want to ask you about, too!"

"If you don't mind, I'll go first," said Clara. "Where did you live before you came here?"

"First I lived with my Aunt Dete and

then with my grandfather on the Wunderhorn. That's in the mountains in Switzerland," Heidi replied.

"It must be a wonderful place to live," Clara said. "In the mountains, I mean!"

"Oh, it is!" answered Heidi. "Just imagine—I didn't even have to wear shoes! And every day I could pick beautiful flowers for Grandfather and tend the goats and play with the animals and—how did that monkey get in here?"

Clara looked at where Heidi was pointing. "My goodness!" she exclaimed. "That's the organ-grinder's monkey! He must have climbed the walls on the ivy!"

The monkey was bouncing from one piece of furniture to another, jabbering and tipping his cap. Suddenly, the two girls heard music coming from below, and the monkey began a merry little dance around the room.

Heidi went to the window to see where the music was coming from. On the sidewalk was the organ-grinder, cranking away at the organ.

"Good morning!" he called, when he saw Heidi at the window. "Is the monkey dancing for you?"

"Oh, yes!" Heidi answered.

"Good!" said the organ-grinder. "He is my world-famous dancing monkey! Remember, though—he's supposed to get a penny when he dances!"

Heidi turned back to the room and told Clara what the organ-grinder said. "Oh, I want him to keep right on dancing," Clara exclaimed. "I have pennies—I'll give him lots of them!" The monkey continued to dance, then stopped in front of Clara, tipping his cap repeatedly. Clara handed him several pennies. The monkey tipped his cap once more, let loose a screech and began to dance again.

"He's wonderful!" Clara cried. "I'd like to keep him dancing forever!" The music from below got louder and faster, and the monkey danced at a furious pace. Clara was trying to keep time clapping her hands, when the door swung open and Frau Rottenmeir, followed by Sebastian, stormed into the room. Frau Rottenmeir spied the monkey at once.

"How did that ugly creature get in here? Sebastian, get him out of here at once!" she yelled.

"At once, Frau Rottenmeir!" Sebastian re-

plied. But that was a lot easier to say than to do—for the monkey, as soon as Sebastian made a move to capture him, began to climb the drapes and perch on top of furniture and light fixtures and make a series of astonishing leaps from one part of the room to another. Things began to get a bit frantic, what with the monkey's antics, Frau Rottenmeir screeching orders at Sebastian and threatening to do terrible things to the monkey and Sebastian trying to flatten the monkey with a broom. Sebastian's normally red face turned quite purple from his exertions. At one point, he raised the broom on high, and roared, "I've got you at last!" Then he brought it down with a crash, only to discover that the broom had swatted Schnoodle instead of the monkey!

Heidi and Clara had moved out of the way into a corner of the room and were nearly collapsing with laughter at the goings-on. Finally, the monkey leaped out of the window and was gone. His departure immediately quieted the uproar in the room.

Frau Rottenmeir gathered up Schnoodle, and said in her very nastiest tone, "Your father will hear of this, young lady! Heidi will

be sent packing the minute he returns! I will see to it personally, you may be sure! Come, Sebastian!" With that, she flounced out of the room, with Sebastian following close behind, as usual.

Heidi looked at Clara and asked, "Do you really think she'll try to have your father send me away?"

"You mustn't mind Frau Rottenmeir too much," replied Clara. "It's the animals, you see. She hates the sight of almost every animal, with the exception of Schnoodle. And because she has to make an excuse for her bad temper, she picks on anyone handy. You're the newest and handiest, so naturally everything is your fault in her eyes."

"But why does she hate animals?" asked Heidi. "I love them! On the Wunderhorn, I have all sorts of animal friends. I even have my very own pet goat!"

"I love them all, too," Clara said. "And I'd love to have a pet of my own. But Frau Rottenmeir says no." Heidi didn't answer this, but she made up her mind to see what she could do about a pet for Clara.

A little while later, Clara said it was time for her to study. Heidi left and went quietly

to the front door. She let herself out without being seen by anyone in the household.

She was standing on the sidewalk, trying to decide which way to go to find a pet, when a voice said, "Hello, there!"

Turning, Heidi saw Willi and his coal wagon, with Gretchen pulling it. "Hello, Willi!" she cried.

"You look like you're lost, even though you're standing right in front of your house!" laughed Willi.

Heidi told him she wanted a pet for Clara but didn't know where to look.

"Oh," Willi said. "That's easy. The butcher's cat just had kittens! I'm sure he'd be glad to see you—he sells the Sesemanns lots of meat! Come, I'll give you a ride to the butcher's! Hop aboard!"

About an hour later, Heidi slipped back into the house, carrying a good-sized basket with a lid on it. She hurried to Clara's room.

"Clara!" she exclaimed. "Just look—I have a surprise for you!" Heidi placed the basket on Clara's lap and said, "Open it!"

Clara lifted the lid of the basket and looked inside. "Kittens!" she gasped. "Four adorable kittens! Where did you find them?"

"The butcher's cat had them," replied Heidi. "Willi told me about them and gave me a ride there. I didn't know which one to take, they were all so cute—so I brought them all!"

"They're so sweet!" Clara cried. She held up one snow-white kitten. "This one is my favourite! I'm going to call him Snowball—and this one is Muffin, and this one is Misty. I can't decide about a name for the last one—he'll just have to wait for his name. We'll keep all of them!"

"But what will Frau Rottenmeir say?" Heidi asked.

"We won't tell her—we'll just have to keep them hidden!" Clara answered. "Isn't this fun?" she went on. "We'll be leading secret lives!" Then Clara and Heidi hid the kittens in the closet in Clara's room, leaving the door open so the kittens would get some air.

In the middle of that night, it began to rain heavily, with lots of wind and thunder and lightning. The crashing of the thunder and the howling of the wind was enough to awaken Heidi. It also awakened Frau Rot-

tenmeir and Sebastian. In the midst of all the other noises, there was a sort of musical crash which seemed to come from the ballroom.

Sebastian leaped from his bed, put on a robe and slippers and came out of his room just in time to see Frau Rottenmeir, who had done exactly as Sebastian had done. In the meantime, Heidi had slipped out of her room, and, keeping herself hidden, watched the butler and housekeeper.

"Sebastian!" said Frau Rottenmeir. "What was that noise?"

Just then, there was another loud crash from the ballroom, followed by a series of tinkling musical notes.

"C-c-c-could it be ghosts, Frau Rottenmeir?" quavered the butler.

"Ghosts? Did you say ghosts?" Frau Rottenmeir's frightened, squeaky voice asked.

"It doesn't have to be ghosts," said Sebastian. "It could be poltergeists!"

There were more tinkling notes from the piano. "I don't like any of this, Sebastian," said Frau Rottenmeir, "particularly ghosts or poltergeists, who are much worse than

ghosts! Ghosts merely clank about and groan, but poltergeists do nasty things to people! But we must find out what is going on! Lead the way—we're going to the ballroom to see what is making this strange music!"

"The ballroom?" Sebastian replied in a scared voice. "But that's where the ghosts and poltergeists are!"

"You coward!" cried Frau Rottenmeir. "Lead the way to the ballroom!"

Through the dark halls they went, their only light coming from a candle held by Sebastian. Heidi followed them, making sure she kept out of sight. Just as they opened the ballroom door, they heard more of the tinkling notes, followed by another loud crash from the piano keys.

"Oh, no!" thought Heidi. "Clara's kittens are loose in the ballroom—jumping on the piano keys—then walking on them! I can't let Frau Rottenmeir and Sebastian find them!"

Frau Rottenmeir went into the ballroom, pulling a reluctant Sebastian behind her. In the confusion, Heidi sneaked in also.

Frau Rottenmeir took the candle from Se-

bastian, walked to the piano and peered closely at the keys. Then she looked inside the piano.

"I can find nothing!" she said. "You see, Sebastian? Where are our ghosts and poltergeists now?"

At that exact moment, two of the kittens clawed their way up the heavy drapery at one of the windows. Heidi, under cover of the darkness in the ballroom, began to shake the drapery to dislodge them. However, she shook a little too hard. The whole drapery came loose and dropped on Heidi's head and shoulders, outlining her head and body and outstretched arms. To make matters worse, there was a flash of lightning, followed by a loud thunderclap.

In the blue-white glare of the lightning, Heidi, covered by the drapes, looked very much like a ghost.

Sebastian let out a strangled roar and Frau Rottenmeir screamed. They both dashed to the door and raced to their rooms. Each of them leaped into bed and spent the rest of the night shivering with the covers pulled over their ears.

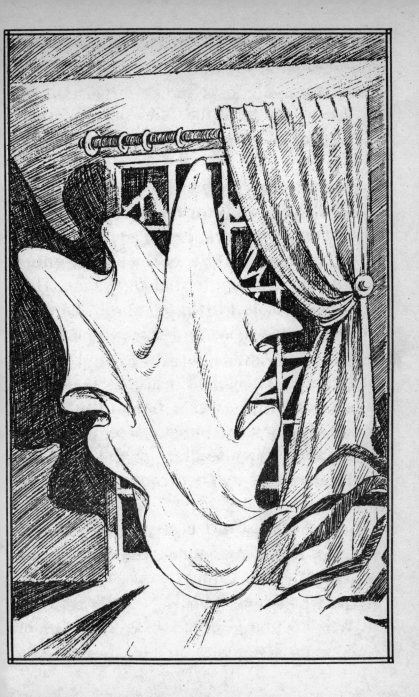

In the morning, Tinette, who had heard the goings-on during the night, told Willi that they had ghosts and poltergeists in the house.

"You saw ghosts and poltergeists?" Willi said.

"No, but we heard them," Tinette answered. "They were in the ballroom!"

At about the same time, Heidi was in Clara's room, telling her what had happened.

"And the whole thing," Heidi finished, "happened because the kittens got loose!"

"Then we mustn't tell anyone!" Clara said. "The kittens are our secret!"

In the meantime, Tinette had led Willi to the ballroom. "You see?" she said. "This is where it all happened!"

"What do they do in such a big room as this?" asked Willi.

"It is for dancing," Tinette answered.

"This whole enormous room is just for dancing?" asked Willi. "It's six times as big as the whole house where I live!"

"What is going on here?" came an angry voice from the doorway. Tinette turned to

see who had spoken. There in the doorway were Frau Rottenmeir and Sebastian.

"I asked Willi to come in and help look for the ghosts," replied Tinette.

"Stupid! There are no ghosts in the daytime!" stormed the housekeeper. "Well! What do you two want?" This last question was to Clara and Heidi, who had just entered the room.

"We wanted to help look for the ghosts, too!" said Clara.

"Nonsense! Don't you know you could hurt yourself looking for ghosts?" replied Frau Rottenmeir. Turning to Tinette, she snarled, "You! Tinette! Get that dust-covered wretch of a Willi out of here!"

"Why are you so upset, Frau Rottenmeir?" Clara said. "Everything is all right, isn't it?"

"No!" cried Frau Rottenmeir. "Everything is all wrong! Nothing is right since that Heidi arrived! She is a bad influence on you, and I won't sleep another minute until she is gone from this house!" Her face, which was usually pale, had become quite red from fury as she said this. But then she gave a

gasp, then a shriek, turned pale again and lifted her skirts, crying, "What is this! What goes on under here!" As she said this, a kitten ran from under her skirt, scurried straight to Heidi and leaped into her arms.

"What is that horrible beast?" Frau Rottenmeir screamed.

"Frau Rottenmeir, it is merely a kitten," said Sebastian.

"You! When I ask you something, then you may answer!" shouted Frau Rottenmeir. "Very well!" she continued, advancing on Heidi. "Where did that—that—thing come from?"

"I got four of them for Clara," Heidi answered.

"Get them out of here! All of them! And at once!" shrieked the housekeeper.

"Oh, no!" cried Clara. "They're my pets and I love them, and I'm going to ask my father to let me keep all of them!"

"They cannot stay!" yelled Frau Rottenmeir. "They are dangerous! They—they will give you the sniffles!" Turning to Heidi, she snarled, "And as for you—you must be taught a lesson. Sebastian! Take her and lock her in the cellar!"

"No!" cried Clara. "You can't do that to Heidi!"

"I can do as I please with her," snapped Frau Rottenmeir. "She is not a member of this family! She is a menace! Take her away!"

Sebastian grasped Heidi firmly by the arm and led her out of the room. As they made their way down the long hall on the way to the cellar stairs, Sebastian said, "So! You like small animals, do you? That is very nice, for where I am taking you, you will find lots of small animals to play with!"

"What kind of small animals?" asked Heidi.

"RATS!" yelled Sebastian. "They will be very happy to play with you—if they don't decide to eat you up first! You will stay in the cellar until Mr. Sesemann comes. The cellar is a fine place to keep troublemakers like you!" By this time they were at the cellar door. Sebastian opened it and gave Heidi a push. "Good night, Heidi!" he said nastily. "Have a lovely time with the small animals!" Then Heidi heard the cellar door slam and a key turn in the lock.

Heidi rattled the doorknob loudly and pounded with her fists, hoping that Tinette would hear her—but to no avail. In despair, Heidi turned slowly to examine her gloomy prison.

By the dim light seeping through a grimy window, Heidi saw nothing but dirt and debris. Broken furniture and empty boxes littered the floor, and an army of spiders had left their webs everywhere. There was also a strong smell of dampness.

Heidi made her way to the window, piled up some boxes and climbed up on them. The dirt on the glass was several years old, but she scraped off enough to peer out.

She called for help, but no one heard—or so she thought. All she could see was part of the backyard—but something in the back yard saw and heard her.

"Whooo!" he called as he flew from his perch in the tree to the cellar window. Hootie peered in and saw his friend was in trouble. But by then, Heidi had given up. She had left the window, found a filthy old blanket, and wrapped herself up in it to try and sleep.

Immediately, Hootie took off in the direc-

tion of the Wunderhorn, flying as fast as his wings would flap.

Heidi woke from her sleep, rubbed her eyes, and looked around. She saw dozens of tiny red lights winking at her. After a closer look, she suddenly realized that the lights were the eyes of the horde of rats in the Sesemann cellar.

"Well!" said Heidi, who had never seen a rat before and who liked all kinds of animals. "There certainly are a lot of you! Do you like living in this dirty cellar?"

Naturally, she got no answer, but there was a lot of squeaking going on, and the rats moved closer to her.

Heidi made up her mind to be brave. She took a deep breath and continued. "I have lots of animal friends on the Wunderhorn—rabbits and goats and squirrels and chipmunks. All sorts of birds, too! Would you like to be friends with me?"

The rats' squeaking increased in volume and they began to form a semicircle around Heidi. But, in a corner of the cellar, there was one rat who didn't join the circle. This one was at least twice the size of the others

and very nasty looking, with long wicked teeth gleaming in the weak light of the cellar. He seemed to be biding his time and planning his next move.

Meanwhile, Hootie was approaching the Wunderhorn. He dived straight down to a landing outside Grandfather's cabin, where Peter was collecting the goats to take to pasture.

It took some time, plus a lot of agitated wing-flapping and loud hooting, but in some mysterious way, Hootie made Peter understand that Heidi was in trouble.

"Hey! Come on!" Peter shouted to all the animals. "We've got to get going in a big hurry! Heidi's in trouble—real trouble in Frankfurt!"

And so, very shortly, a strange looking group set out to save Heidi. First came Peter on his high-wheeled bicycle. The bicycle was pulling a wagon full of an odd assortment of animals: goats, rabbits, squirrels and chipmunks. Even Gruffle and Great Turk came along. High overhead, Hootie flew, leading the way.

In the cellar, Heidi was still telling the rats all about life on the Wunderhorn. The rats seemed to enjoy what they were hearing and appeared friendly. They squeaked furiously whenever Heidi stopped talking.

Heidi had talked, almost non-stop, for several days before the big rat decided it was time to take action. Drawing himself up to his full height, he scurried to a point in front of the other rats and began to pace up and down, squeaking angrily. The other rats stirred uneasily, looking from the big rat to Heidi and back again. As the king rat continued to stir up the others, their attitude toward Heidi changed from friendly interest to outright anger and menace.

"My goodness!" thought Heidi. "That big one seems to be working up the others to do something dreadful—to me!"

Finally, the rats were worked up to a very angry mood, ready to attack.

Luckily, by that time, Peter and his collection of animals were following Hootie among the tall buildings of Frankfurt. At

last, Hootie dropped down from high overhead and perched on a flight of steep steps.

"Here!" yelled Peter. "This must be the
house!"

Hootie flew to the cellar window and
flapped his wings against the glass. Peter
and the animals were close behind. Suddenly, they stopped. How would they get in?

Peter realized Heidi must be in the cellar
and was going to break the window with a
stone.

"No need!" said a voice. Turning, Peter
saw a young man and a horse and wagon
loaded with coal.

"I'm a friend of Heidi's!" shouted Peter.
"She's locked in the cellar—and it's full of
hungry rats."

"So am I a friend of Heidi!" exclaimed
Willi. "We have to save her!"

Willi swung his coal chute to the cellar
window, gave a push, and the whole window
fell in, just as the rats attacked!

Down the chute came Willi and Peter,
with the animals not far behind. After Gruf-

fle and Great Turk took care of the big rat, the others lost interest and disappeared.

Heidi hugged all her friends at the same time and took them upstairs to meet Clara.

After things had quieted down, Heidi said to Clara, "I'm sure you meant well, Clara, but if you don't mind, I want to go home to the Wunderhorn!"

"I'll miss you so much, Heidi!" Clara cried. "Why can't we be together?"

"We can, if you come home with me," replied Heidi. "And I know the mountain air will be good for you!"

"I wish I could!" sighed Clara. "It would be such fun!"

"You can!" exclaimed Heidi. "Just make up your mind, and we'll leave right now!"

"Very well, then," Clara said firmly. "I *will* do it! First I will write a note for my father—and then—we go to Switzerland! Willi! Come up here, please!"

Willi dashed upstairs and brought Clara and the four kittens down in her wheelchair, accompanied by Tinette. Then everyone piled into Willi's wagon and Gretchen pulled them away at a fast clip.

The next day, Clara's father arrived and found Clara's note, which read: "Dear Father: I have gone to see the mountains with Heidi. Please don't worry—I'll be very careful, and I'm sure Heidi's grandfather will bring me back. Your loving daughter, Clara."

"What is the meaning of this?" he said sternly to Sebastian and Frau Rottenmeir. "Who is this Heidi—and what mountains?"

Frau Rottenmeir explained what had happened and where the mountains were and then admitted what they had done to Heidi.

"I will see that you two are punished!" he shouted as he raced out the door. "But later—after I have found Clara!" He hurried to the stables and saddled his fastest horse.

Back at the house, Sebastian looked at Frau Rottenmeir. "I think," he said, "that if we wish to escape something very bad happening to us, we should leave right away!"

"You are right, Sebastian! Let's be far from here when they all return!" replied Frau Rottenmeir. And gone they were in a very few minutes.

Not very long after that, Heidi and her friends arrived at the foot of the mountains. "Look there!" Heidi said, pointing to a spot high up in the mountains. "That big one is the Wunderhorn, where I live!"

"Oh, Heidi, it's beautiful!" cried Clara. "Just think! I might never have seen these mountains without your help!"

A short while later, they came to a point beyond which the wagon could not go. Here Willi and Tinette said good-bye, telling Heidi, Clara and Peter that they were going to see Willi's family and get married. Everyone said good-bye, and then the rest started up the mountain, with Peter pushing Clara in her chair.

They had reached a small meadow, when Clara said, "Can I stay here and just look for a while? I've never seen anything like this!"

Heidi and Peter agreed—and raced on to see Grandfather. Far below them Mr. Sesemann was on his way on horseback.

Grandfather, of course, was overjoyed to see Heidi and made an enormous fuss over her. After a few minutes, Heidi said, "Peter,

maybe we'd better go back down to bring Clara up here!"

In the meadow, Clara had opened the basket and let the kittens out. Snowball was quite curious and wandered to the end of the meadow where he saw a butterfly and gave chase.

Suddenly, he slipped! He just barely managed to hook his claws on a slender branch and then dangled helplessly over the cliff at the meadow's edge.

Clara screamed for help, but knew no one could save Snowball but her. Without hesitating, she deliberately toppled over out of her wheelchair and began a painful crawl to her pet.

High up on the mountainside, a sharp-eyed hawk watched the helpless kitten dangle so temptingly below. Instantly, he dove from his nest with a piercing cry.

Clara got to Snowball just seconds before the hawk did. She flailed at the hawk and landed a hard blow to its head. Shrieking angrily, the hawk retreated.

Clara plucked Snowball from where he dangled over the cliff and, clutching the

shivering kitten tightly, began a laborious crawl back to her wheelchair.

Once there, she managed to get to her knees. Then, exerting every bit of strength she possessed, she tried to get into the chair. But she pushed too hard with her arms and suddenly, she was standing!

She had no idea how it had happened and was afraid no one would believe it.

Then it seemed as if everyone arrived at once. Peter and Heidi were running, with Grandfather lumbering behind and Mr. Sesemann arrived on his horse. Mr. Sesemann gathered Clara in his arms for a big hug.

"Please put me down, Father," Clara said "I would like to try to walk now!"

Clara's father looked at her in wonderment, and perhaps a little fear. Then he lowered her gently until she was standing once more. Once on her feet, Clara began to take cautious steps. First slowly, then faster and faster, until she was almost dancing around the meadow.

"I can't believe my eyes!" cried Mr. Sesemann.

"It is the mountains!" exclaimed Grandfather. "Everything does better up here! Let's all go to the cabin! This is a day for celebration—Heidi is safely home—and Clara can walk again!"

Clara said, "How can I ever thank you, Heidi and Peter and all of you?"

"Don't even think about it, Clara," Heidi replied. "Remember—that's what real friends are for!"